First American Edition 2016
Kane Miller, A Division of EDC Publishing

For information contact:
Kane Miller, A Division of EDC Publishing
P.O. Box 470663
Tulsa, OK 74147-0663
www.kanemiller.com
www.edcpub.com
www.usbornebooksandmore.com

Library of Congress Control Number: 2015953927

Printed and bound in the United States of America
1 2 3 4 5 6 7 8 9 10

ISBN: 978-1-61067-507-9

ON THE BALL

.... ".___ ... '.___ ___' ___' '.___ ....

___ ___ ___'.___' ".___' '.___ '.___ '.___"'.___ ___'.

Kane Miller
A DIVISION OF EDC PUBLISHING

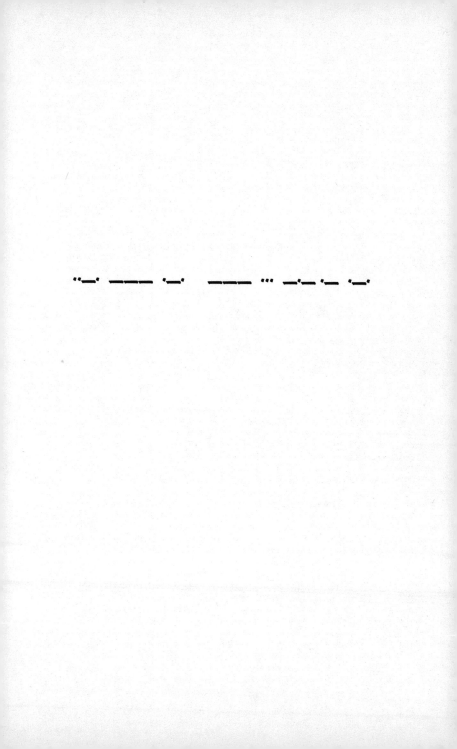

Chapter 1

Emma Jacks had never run so much in her life. Her chest heaved and her legs ached. She wasn't sure she could keep running and keep kicking the soccer ball at the same time. But she had to. She was right by the goal and a goal would put the girls in front of the boys. Just as Emma thought she would have to stop, one of her best friends, Hannah, sprinted up beside her.

"Em, here, pass the ball!" yelled Hannah.

Emma kicked the ball and it shot across the field. Emma thought she had kicked it straight to Hannah so was surprised when she saw Oskar running in the opposite direction with the ball. Emma's heart sank: she had kicked the ball to Oskar.

"Bad luck, Em," cried Hannah, as she chased after Oskar.

Bad luck, nothing, thought Emma. *I just can't kick straight! Oskar was miles away from Hannah!*

But there was no time to think about that now. Isi was down at the other end of the field and had skillfully taken the ball back from Oskar. She was now powering back up the field toward Emma. Isi kicked the ball to Hannah, who was running fast. Just as Dougall caught up, Hannah kicked the ball toward Emma.

"It's yours, Em," she called. "Head it into goal. You can do it."

I can? Emma tried to get ready. She watched the ball. She watched it coming toward her, high in the sky, in front of the goal. Emma got ready to jump. She closed her eyes. She could see it all in her mind: she was going to jump up and meet the ball and, with just a little nudge of the head, she was going to guide it into goal. Well, that was the plan. Somebody should have told Emma's head the plan.

Emma jumped up, aiming her head at the ball, waiting for contact. No contact. She turned her head and watched as the ball sailed past her and back onto Oskar's foot. Oskar ran, then passed it to Edvard, who kicked it into the far goal.

Ms. Tenga blew her whistle. Boys 1, Girls 0. Boys ecstatic. Emma not impressed.

The goalie threw the ball back into play for the girls. Isi took it, but was soon tackled by Edvard. Isi did well to get the ball free, but she couldn't control where it went and she kicked it to an empty part of the field. The closest girl to the ball was Nema who, unfortunately, seemed to be braiding her hair.

"Nema," shouted Isi, "the ball! Nema, get the ball. It's the round thing coming toward you!"

"Oh, what, this?" said Nema, picking up the ball.

Ms. Tenga's whistle blew.

"Foul. Boys' ball," cried Ms. Tenga. "Nema, you can't pick the ball up with your hands. You have to kick it with your feet."

"Oh, sorry, Ms. Tenga," said Nema, who then in a low voice muttered so her teacher couldn't hear her, "stupid rule, stupid boys' game."

Edvard took off with the ball but, just as it looked as if the boys were going to score another goal, Hannah swooped in and took possession. She quickly passed the ball to Emma, who was waiting on the side. Emma ran a bit farther up the field before passing to Isi, who shrugged off Oskar and kicked it high to Cat, who was right in front of goal. Cat leapt up, as if she was about to take off, and with a perfect header, she sent the ball into the goal.

Ms. Tenga blew her whistle again. Girls 1, Boys 1. The girls leapt all over each other in delight. Emma was thrilled and almost forgot about her missed header.

There was time for just one more play. They were still close to the girls' goal so Emma was hopeful they'd score again.

Callum threw the ball in for the boys. He was

aiming for Edvard but Isi, seeing what Callum was doing, snuck in front and took the ball. Callum tackled hard, but Isi managed to kick the ball to Hannah, who only just beat Edvard to it. Again Hannah kicked the ball up high toward Emma.

"This time, Em," Hannah shouted, "head this one in."

Emma went up again. She stretched her neck and pushed with her head. Contact. The ball flew through the air. It went high, much too high, over the goal and out of bounds.

Ms. Tenga blew the whistle.

"Bad luck, Emma. Good try," cried Ms. Tenga. "Great game everyone! That's it for today. Now quickly into the locker rooms."

Everyone rushed off, except Emma was a bit slower than the others. She was angry with herself for missing both those headers. She felt she had let the team down. Hannah must have noticed her friend looking sad and came up and put an arm around her.

"Cheer up," she said.

Then Isi bounded up to them. Isi was, as always, excited.

"How fun was that!" she exclaimed. "And we nearly won. Those boys were so sure that they would beat us by heaps and it was a tie. Yay, us!"

"Yay, you, maybe," said Emma. "I can't believe I missed two headers. Maybe I shouldn't try out for the school team."

"No, you have to," cried Isi. "How cool will it be if we all play together? And this year, the team is going to have team shirts with our names on them! You have to be on the team, Em, you just have to be!"

"I have to make the team first," said Emma glumly.

"Why would anyone want to be on the soccer team?" said Nema, who had walked up alongside them. "It's a boys' sport."

Ms. Tenga was coming up behind the girls. She must have heard their conversation.

"Don't be silly, Nema, soccer is one of the largest girls' sports in the world. And don't be so hard on yourself, Emma. You played really well today. Headers take a lot of practice. Keep trying, stay on the ball and you could really shine."

Emma blushed. *On the ball. Gee whizz, lemonfizz, I should be good at that,* she thought.

And she should. After all when she wasn't Emma Jacks, schoolgirl and not very confident soccer player, she was Special Agent EJ12, code-cracker for the under-twelve division of the secret agency **SHINE**. And a secret agent always had to stay on the ball.

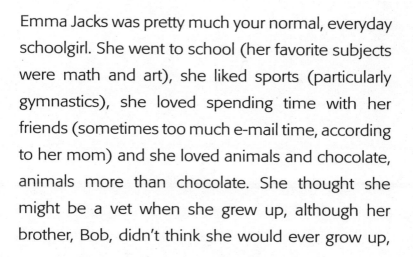

Emma Jacks was pretty much your normal, everyday schoolgirl. She went to school (her favorite subjects were math and art), she liked sports (particularly gymnastics), she loved spending time with her friends (sometimes too much e-mail time, according to her mom) and she loved animals and chocolate, animals more than chocolate. She thought she might be a vet when she grew up, although her brother, Bob, didn't think she would ever grow up, which gives you an idea of how irritating Bob was.

Emma worried about things sometimes, normal things. Sometimes she worried about friends (and mean girls not being friends), sometimes she worried about school and quite often she worried about whether she would be able to do something well. Like soccer. So, Emma Jacks was pretty normal, very normal in fact—except for the spy thing. Except for being one of **SHINE**'s best secret agents.

SHINE was a worldwide secret organization that stopped evil plans, particularly those of the *SHADOW* organization. *SHADOW* was as bad as **SHINE** was good and they seemed to be always launching new evil schemes. *SHADOW* used secret messages to send instructions to their agents and they were always inventing new ways to make sure those messages couldn't be intercepted or decoded.

Luckily, **SHINE**'s agents were very good at cracking new codes and foiling *SHADOW* plans. Agents like EJ12. She enjoyed looking at the code and picking the clue within it, finding the thing that would let her decode it. This was a problem she enjoyed—and she was good at it. She had a good head for secret messages and codes. She was pretty good at the missions too and was awarded lots of points in the **SHINE** Shining Stars, the Spy of the Year competition.

She just wished she had a good head for soccer as well.

Chapter •2

That afternoon at home Emma was practicing her headers with her older brother, Bob. Strangely, Bob was being nice to her. Although she was suspicious, she needed the help with her soccer and Bob, she had to admit, was pretty good at soccer. Their puppy, Pip, was also pretty good and was joining in chasing the ball all over the yard. It seemed everyone was better than Emma at soccer.

"When you see the ball coming," said Bob, "just reach up, stretch your neck and nudge the ball with your forehead. Here, throw the ball up toward me and I'll show you."

Emma threw the ball up high toward Bob. His eyes on the ball, he leapt and stretched to meet the ball and then, with his forehead, he pushed it back to her.

"See, easy!" said Bob.

"Maybe for you," replied Emma grumpily.

"Try again," said Bob, as he threw the ball up.

As the ball came toward her, Emma looked toward where it was going and jumped. But she jumped just a little too late and the ball hit the ground.

"Nearly, it just takes practice," said Bob. "You'll get it. Maybe we can do some more tomorrow."

Bob went inside leaving Emma holding the ball and wondering if any amount of practice would help her headers. It was so frustrating: she could catch balls really well, but she just couldn't seem to get headers right—and if she couldn't do a header, how was she going to get on the school soccer team? She would have to practice all weekend if she was going to have a chance at the tryouts when school went back.

The weekend. That reminded Emma. What was she going to do? It was a long weekend, but all her friends were going away. Elle and her family were going to visit her grandmother, Isi and her family were going camping and Hannah and her sister were going to stay with their cousins. Even Bob was going to a soccer camp with his team. She wouldn't be able to practice with him. Things were desperate if you were going to miss your brother. The long weekend was going to be so boring.

Piinngg!

Emma jumped. That was no ordinary ping and it came from her very not ordinary phone. It was a special-issue SHINE phone that looked a bit like a game console and a bit like a touch phone. It had lots of normal applications, but it also had special SHINE spy apps, including a special SHINE message system that alerted their agents to report in. It was this system that had just sent Emma a message.

Emma took out her phone and opened the

message. She was surprised at what she saw: it didn't look like the usual SHINE message alert.

IT WON'T MEAN A THING IF YOU USE A WINGDING.

What does this mean? wondered Emma. *Is the first line a motto?* **SHINE** liked mottoes and they had lots, but what did "It won't mean a thing if you use a wingding" mean? It certainly didn't mean a thing to Emma. She couldn't make heads or tails of it.

It has to be a clue, thought Emma. *It has to be telling me how to crack the code.* She read the top line again.

What's a wingding? Emma asked herself. *I've heard that word before, but where?* Then she remembered. *On the computer, it's a font on the computer.*

Emma liked fonts, she liked writing her name in different fonts. She liked finding fonts that expressed different styles and different moods. There could be bold, strong fonts and more pretty, girly fonts and there could be just plain nutty fonts. There could be fonts for when Emma felt happy and fonts for when she felt sad. Sometimes Emma made up new fonts herself with a pen, but she also liked choosing different ones on the computer. She had quite a few that were her special favorites.

Emma Jacks
Emma Jacks
Emma Jacks
Emma Jacks
Emma Jacks
Emma Jacks

I think I remember a wingdings font, said Emma to herself. She scrolled to her word app and keyed her name. She then highlighted it and pressed "choose font" and scrolled through her options. *Wingdings, starting with W, should be toward the end,* thought Emma.

"There you are," she said, pressing "wingdings." Now her name looked like a cross between hieroglyphics and a comic book.

☜○○♋ ☺♋♍♏&✦

Emma smiled to herself. *Emma Jacks, your head may be a bit slow with the ball, but it is fast with the codes.* She went back to the **SHINE** message, highlighted the text and chose another font. "It may not mean a thing if you use wingdings, but if I use this font, let's see what happens," Emma said to herself as she pressed another of her favorite fonts.

Well done on cracking the

code, Agent E J12!

Come and improve your spy skills

at a weekend training camp.

Report via mission tube

Friday afternoon.

Reply YES to confirm.

A weekend training camp with **SHINE**? Emma was excited. What would that be like? Where would it be? What would they do? Who else would be there? Would she know anyone? Most importantly, would she be able to go? Before Emma could think of any more questions, her phone went again.

Piinngg!

There was another message on her phone, but this one was from her mom.

```
GOT CAMP MESSAGE.
OK TO GO.
YOU'LL HAVE A BALL.
MOM X
```

Emma's mom used to be a **SHINE** agent and she now helped Emma on her missions. **SHINE** must have sent her mom a message too—after all, agents in the under-twelve division needed their parents' permission to go on missions. And now

Emma had it. She pressed "reply" on the **SHINE** message system and keyed in her answer.

YES

As she pressed "send," Emma smiled. Not only had she solved the code, she had solved her long weekend problem as well.

Chapter · 3

It was the last class of the last day before the long weekend. Emma's bag was packed with the things she needed for camp. Packing had been easy because **SHINE** had said there was no need to bring clothes, just toiletries. Emma couldn't wait for school to finish.

Finally the bell went. Everyone cheered and ran out the door. Emma rushed out with Isi, Elle and Hannah but knew she would have to make her way to report in to the **SHINE** Mission Tube.

SHINE had a secret network of tunnels that

allowed agents to be brought to HQ quickly and without anyone knowing. Different agents used different tubes. Each tube needed to be somewhere the agent went frequently yet a place where the entry could be concealed. Emma's Mission Tube started in one of the girls' bathrooms at school. Emma understood it made sense, but that didn't mean it wasn't a bit embarrassing.

Although Emma's closest friends knew she was a secret agent, and sometimes helped on missions as part of BEST (Brains, Expertise, Support and Tips), the **SHINE** agent phone assist scheme, they weren't allowed to discuss missions. They had, however, worked out their own secret code so Emma could let her friends know when she had to leave. As Isi, Hannah and Elle made their way to the bus, Emma dropped back a bit.

"Come on, Em, we'll miss the bus," said Hannah.

"I'll see you guys," she said to her friends. "I need to go to the bathroom."

"Oh, we can wait, Em," said Elle.

"No, Elle, I'm going OM," whispered Emma.
OM meant On Mission. Well, this time it wasn't really a mission, but it would have been too complicated to explain.

"Right," said Elle. "See you next week then. Good luck."

"Bye, Em!" cried Isi. "Don't forget to practice. I can't wait to see our names on those soccer shirts!"

"Me too. Bye, Han, bye, Isi, see you, Elle," cried Emma, as she turned and headed toward the bathroom.

Emma pushed the door to the girls' bathroom open. First checking no one else was there, she then turned on the hand dryers and went to the last stall on the right, closing and locking the door behind her. She put down the toilet seat, sat down and flipped open the toilet paper holder. This would have been an odd thing to do, except it was no ordinary toilet paper holder, it concealed the **SHINE** Mission Tube access pad. There was a small socket on the side of the holder. Emma pushed her phone into it and waited. There was a beep. Emma entered her pin code and then removed her phone. There was another beep and then words flashed on her phone screen.

WELCOME BACK EJ12.
HOLD ON!

EJ held on to the edge of the toilet seat and counted to three. On three, the wall behind the toilet spun around, with the toilet and EJ attached. On the count of four, EJ was sitting on a beanbag at the top of a giant tunnel slide. On the count of five, the wall spun back and a protective shield covered EJ and the beanbag. She had entered the **SHINE** Mission Tube. EJ then pushed 1 on her phone and WHOOOOOOOOOSH! she sped down what looked like a giant pipe, shiny and brightly lit.

Normally EJ stopped at the Code Room, but this time she sped past it until she came to a stop outside two large metal doors. Next to the doors was a small keypad. EJ stood up and again keyed in her pin code and waited for the security check. The check changed each time. Sometimes it would be fingerprints, sometimes an eye scan, once EJ even had to sing a song—that was a little embarrassing. The checks were constantly changing to ensure that no one could break into SHINE HQ. EJ wondered what it would be this time.

EJ stood still and waited. And waited. Nothing happened. She moved a bit closer to the doors. *Perhaps I'm not in the right position*, she thought.

"Please don't move," a digital voice instructed. "Head recognition test about to commence."

There was a whirring noise coming from above and as EJ looked up, she saw the light in the ceiling slide to one side and what looked like a baseball cap descending toward her. As it came closer she could see that it was a baseball cap, black with the SHINE logo on the front. EJ stood still while the cap lowered onto her head. She felt it tighten as it seemed to grip on to the sides of her head. There was a buzzing noise for three seconds before EJ felt the cap loosen and then lift and go back up and into the ceiling.

"Head scan complete. Agent identity confirmed," said the digital voice. "Access to headquarters granted, EJ12. Enter briefing room."

EJ smiled. Head scan for headquarters access. Good one.

The silver doors slid open, revealing the **SHINE** operations room. There were workstations and computer screens everywhere and a back wall filled with monitors flashing images from all over the world. In the middle of it all, as always, stood A1, the head of **SHINE**.

"Welcome back, EJ12," said A1, smiling broadly. "It is good to see you again."

Normally A1 wore a black suit and crisp white shirt, but this afternoon she was in distinctly more casual clothes—sports shoes, gray tracksuit pants, white T-shirt and, over the top, a gray hoodie with the **SHINE** logo across the front. It looked like a warm, comfy hoodie and EJ wondered whether she would get a **SHINE** hoodie as well. She hoped so.

"Your **SHINE** hoodie and the rest of your training gear is waiting for you in dressing room 1, EJ," said A1, who had a disconcerting ability to know what you were thinking. "Leave your school clothes there and we will send them home to your mother, washed and ready for school next week."

Mom will love **SHINE** *for that,* thought EJ. Her mom didn't like doing laundry. Actually EJ didn't know anyone who did.

"Now be as quick as you can please, EJ12, we need to leave soon."

EJ went into the first of three dressing rooms at the other end of the room. On the chair inside were some tracksuit pants, a white T-shirt, sneakers and socks, yellow shorts with aqua trim and a **SHINE** hoodie. There was also a **SHINE** identity card on a cord for EJ to put around her neck and a backpack with a special-issue **SHINE** water bottle. In next to no time, EJ was out of her school clothes and in her training gear. She came out of the dressing room and went back to where A1 was waiting for her.

"That was nice and quick, EJ. I think we are ready to go. We will have a full briefing at the camp and our train is ready to leave. We were just waiting on you and one other agent. She is just getting changed as well."

EJ looked around and noticed that one of the dressing room doors was shut.

"Ah yes, here she is," continued A1. "And I think you two know each other."

E J turned around as a small, reddish-blond haired girl came out of the middle dressing room. A smile burst onto EJ's face, and the girl grinned back.

"CC12!" cried EJ.

"EJ12," cried the girl.

"CC, are you going to the training camp too? That's so cool!" cried E J, who had met Agent CC12 when they were both on a mission inside a chocolate cake bakery. Any butterflies E J had had about going to the camp flew away when she saw CC.

CC gave EJ a big hug.

"Okay, girls, I am pleased you are so happy to see each other, but we need to keep moving," said

A1, smiling. "There will be plenty of time to talk on the train. Agents EJ12 and CC12, our train is ready."

And with that A1 pushed a button under the counter behind her. The wall at the end of the operations room slid back to reveal another Mission Tube and a silver bullet train.

"All aboard the **SHINE** camp express!" said A1.

Chapter •4

EJ12 remembered the **SHINE** bullet train, indeed, she had driven it once on a mission. Today she was a passenger with about twenty other agents of different ages. They were all dressed in the **SHINE**-issue gray tracksuit pants and hoodies. Everyone seemed to be talking excitedly at once: it was just like on the bus going to camp.

A1 went up to the front and gave the driver the all clear to depart. As EJ and CC walked toward the back of the train, they saw another girl that looked about their age, sitting alone.

"Can we sit with you?" EJ asked.

"Sure," replied the girl, smiling. "I'm Agent KM12, under-twelve fast-transportation division and general missions."

EJ sat next to her. "I'm EJ12, under-twelve code-cracking division and general missions."

"And I'm CC12," said CC. "Under-twelve surveillance division and general missions."

"We've got most areas covered," laughed KM. "Between us we should be able to take on anything."

The girls giggled and began to talk. As they all had the same security clearance, they could talk about their missions. Sometimes the hardest thing about being a secret agent was having to keep it a secret.

"What's been your favorite mission so far, EJ?" asked KM.

"It would have to be the chocolate cake bakery one," said EJ, smiling at CC. "Not only did I finally figure out how to bake a cupcake, but I met CC. It was fun doing part of a mission with someone else. Although, actually, the Antarctica one was pretty amazing. I saw thousands of baby penguins and rode the **SHINE** mobile."

"I *love* **SHINE** mobiles," cried KM. "Have you used them on open seas yet? You can go almost 100 miles per hour. It is awesome!"

"That sounds pretty fast," said CC. "I normally have to stay really still and watch things. I wonder what would happen if we switched missions once?"

"I'm not sure that would be a good idea," said EJ. "I get the feeling KM is not so good at standing still."

The girls laughed again.

"What's your best spy charm?" asked CC, twisting her charm bracelet.

Every **SHINE** agent had a special-issue bracelet of silver charms that were in fact CHARMs, Clever Hidden Accessories with Release Mechanism. **SHINE** agents often needed special tools and gadgets to help them on their missions, but they couldn't carry a whole lot of equipment around with them all the time. Not only would it be too heavy, but also it would attract attention. The clever team of inventors at the **SHINE** laboratory had invented a way to shrink gadgets so that they could be worn as charms on a bracelet. Who would ever suspect that on an agents' wrist was an ice pick, baby penguin food, a camera hidden in a plastic cupcake, a skeleton key and even spider repellent? A simple twist of the charm released the gadget to its real size. Another twist would re-shrink it back to a charm or, if necessary, there was a small button that could be pushed to make the item decompose to nothing.

"Do you have this one?" asked CC, holding a little flashlight charm. "It looks small, but it is a really powerful flashlight."

E J, who wasn't that keen on night missions, would have loved that charm. "I haven't got that one, but I have got glow rope—it is really long and glows in the dark. You can use it to leave a trail at night."

"I have a rope charm," said KM, "but it doesn't glow."

"My rope charm doesn't glow either," said CC. "I wonder if we can upgrade?"

The girls compared spy charms, then apps on their phones and then swapped music from their spy-pods. It was fun. KM12 reminded EJ a lot of Isi. KM was also enthusiastic about everything and talked excitedly at a hundred miles an hour—no wonder she was in the fast-transportation division.

The girls were talking so much that they didn't notice that the **SHINE** bullet train had left the Mission Tube tunnel and was now speeding up into the mountains.

The girls only stopped talking when the train pulled in at a small railway siding. They had arrived. But where were they? There was no railway station and no sign, just a narrow wooden platform by the tracks in the middle of the bush.

The doors of the train opened and the agents stepped out. The air was fresh and EJ breathed in the sweet smell of the eucalyptus trees as she listened to the chatter of birds and rustle of leaves in the light wind.

"All right, **SHINE** agents, everyone follow me," cried A1. "Single file, please and as quick as you can."

"Where do you think we are, EJ?" asked KM.

"I don't know," replied EJ, "but we were on the train for a long time and look across there, there is nothing but trees and hills."

"It's beautiful," said CC. "Don't you feel like we are the only people for miles?"

"I guess that's the point," said EJ. "We can train with no one knowing we are here."

EJ, KM and CC followed the other agents and pushed through the bushes and stepped onto a dirt walking track that sloped down the mountain. The agents walked along, with tall straight trees towering over them on either side. After a while, there were fewer trees and the track leveled out as they came to a large natural clearing. In the middle of the clearing, the grass had been cut so it was like a sports field. At the edge of the field was a long wooden cabin with wooden benches and tables outside. Six smaller cabins were next to the long cabin and on the other side of the field, close to all the trees, there was a run of enclosures. EJ wondered what was kept in there.

A high wire fence surrounded the whole area and there was a double gate that opened automatically as the group walked toward it. As the agents walked in, some older agents came out of the large cabin. EJ smiled as she recognized C2C, the sea captain, REV1, the **SHINE** driving ace, CO45, the code scientist and IQ400, **SHINE**'s chief inventor. There was also a woman coming from the enclosures at the far end. EJ didn't recognize her, but she knew the beautiful husky dog she had on a leash—it was one of the huskies that EJ had rescued on her Antarctica mission. A1 had said that they would be retrained at a **SHINE** camp.

All the senior agents joined A1 as she stood at the front of the group. EJ hoped that she would be able to spend some time with them.

"Welcome, everyone," cried A1.

There were some barks and yelps coming from

the pens.

"Welcome to both dog and human agents," laughed A1. "And, of course, we must not forget our puppies."

EJ, KM and CC all looked at each other and then squealed in a very non-secret agent way.

Puppies!

Chapter •5

"Welcome to the Mount Globe **SHINE** training camp," repeated A1, "**SHINE**'s top secret training facility. No one knows we are here."

And then, EJ noticed, A1 looked across to IQ400. Was that a worried look on A1's face or was EJ imagining it?

"Over the next two days," continued A1, "you will work on some of your special agent skills. The older agents will spend the time hiking and camping on the far side of Mount Globe with Agents CO45, REV1 and C2C. They will leave at nightfall. The under-twelve division will remain here with me,

Agents 1Q400 and BRK9, head of our dog division."

"Oh, that's disappointing. I was hoping we would be going camping," whispered CC.

"The under-twelves should not feel disappointed," continued A1.

"How *does* she do that?" whispered CC again.

"The under-twelves," continued A1, "will practice for their dirt bike licenses and they will also work with BRK9 to assist in puppy training. Some puppies were found abandoned near the camp and we have adopted them. They are training extremely well. And, on the last evening we will have a night-time drill with our spy-talkers."

"I totally take that back about being disappointed," said CC, smiling broadly. EJ and KM smiled back.

"Finally, you will all have a session with our chief inventor, Agent IQ400, who will show you some new charms we have in development. I need not remind you all how top secret this work is: *SHADOW* would do anything to get their hands on these new inventions. They would also like these training charms. Agent IQ400, will you please demonstrate the charms to our agents?"

"Certainly, A1."

A tall woman about the same age as EJ's mom stepped forward. It was Agent IQ400. Tall and dressed in **SHINE** training gear, Agent IQ400 had brown hair tied back in a sensible ponytail, but she also wore some very un-sensible and fun yellow-rimmed glasses. She held a large black briefcase out in front of her. Agent IQ400 pushed a button on its handle and four legs shot out of the case to make, as IQ400 turned it over, a table, a briefcase table.

"That's cool," KM whispered to EJ.

EJ nodded and wondered if you could get school bags like that. It could be good for homework.

IQ cleared her throat and began to speak. "Thank you, A1, and hello, fellow agents. I have here two training charms, but in order to demonstrate them, I need a volunteer."

Along with every other agent, EJ, KM and CC's hands shot up. EJ couldn't hide her smile as IQ picked her.

"Now," said IQ, holding up a silver charm in the shape of a sports shoe, "with this charm, there is an extra twist. Literally. You twist once to the left and once to the right and wait a few seconds and yes, here they are, one shoe for the left and one shoe for the right." IQ was holding a pair of sports shoes. "These shoes mold perfectly to fit each agent's feet," she said, passing the shoes to EJ, who put them on. As she pulled on the laces, EJ felt the shoes vibrate and push in and around her foot until they fit snugly.

"Now," said IQ, "these are, of course, no ordinary training shoes. How high can you jump in the air, Agent EJ12?" she asked.

"Maybe a foot and a half," replied EJ.

"Let's see if we can improve on that," said IQ. "You will see there are three buttons on the side of the left shoe. EJ12, please press the green button with the upward arrow and then jump."

EJ pressed the button and jumped.

BOING!

EJ shot nearly nine feet into the air. It was as if she was wearing springs. The bounce so caught EJ off guard that she nearly fell over when she landed. Everyone gasped. EJ steadied herself then jumped again, this time bouncing even higher and with greater control. For a moment, she could see over the roofs of the camp cabins.

"These are awesome!" cried EJ, as she made a perfect landing. Her gymnastics coach would have been happy.

"They are rather, aren't they?" said IQ. "Thank you, EJ12, you may return to the group. There is also a button for running on water, but I really think we should be in our swimming gear to try that one. And, finally, there is a button for increased running speed. Who would like to demonstrate that one?"

KM's hand shot up. She looked like she was going to burst if IQ didn't pick her.

A1 noticed the color KM's face was turning and smiled as she spoke to IQ. "I think you better pick Agent KM12 from our fast-transportation division."

IQ smiled. "KM12?"

KM bounded forward and took the charm from IQ. She twisted it left and right and then put on her shoes. Once they had adjusted to her feet, she looked up at IQ, waiting.

"Okay," said IQ. "Now press the pink button with the lightning bolt on it and run to the front gate of the camp please, KM12."

KM pressed the button. There was a whirring noise from the shoes, like a small motor. As KM began to run, the shoes seem to propel her forward, faster, much faster. She looked a bit wobbly on the shoes for the first couple of steps but soon found her balance. In what seemed like no time at all, KM had run to the gate and was back standing next to IQ, hardly out of breath at all.

"The **SHINE** athletic record for that distance is 30 seconds with normal running shoes. With these new turbo shoes, Agent KM12 did it in just 7.5 seconds. The shoes give a 30-second burst of motorized speed. After the 30 seconds you have to wait another ten seconds before you can speed again. Thank you, KM, you may keep those shoes on."

KM beamed. EJ wondered if KM would ever take the shoes off again.

"Now, our final charm is a training whistle." IQ took out a charm in the shape of a sports whistle. She twisted it and then took something from the side of the whistle and put it in one ear. IQ then held the whistle up to her lips and blew. Nothing happened. There was no sound, but EJ did notice that the husky standing with Agent BRK9 suddenly looked up and tilted its head toward IQ400.

"Can anyone hear that?" she asked.

Everyone looked blankly at IQ and shook their heads.

Hear what? wondered EJ.

"Okay, try this. Agent CC, come up here please and activate this whistle charm."

CC went up and took the whistle charm from IQ and twisted.

"Now take the small plug from the side and place it in one of your ears. Then tell me what you hear."

IQ blew on her whistle again. This time the

husky stood up and began barking.

"Wow," said CC shaking her head, "that's really high-pitched."

"It certainly is," said IQ, "because this is a high frequency whistle. We know that dogs have much better hearing than humans and can hear more sounds, more frequencies than we can. This whistle makes a higher frequency sound that dogs can hear and, if we use the plug in the whistle, we can hear the noise as well. This charm is very useful when working with our dog agents: different types and numbers of whistles can mean different commands. You might also use it to communicate with another agent—as long as they are wearing the plug, of course. Now, everyone, please come up and collect your charms."

The agents filed up and took one of each of the charms from the briefcase. As they were attaching them to their bracelets, A1 started talking.

"Please activate your shoe charms immediately. You will need them for our first exercise, a cross-country run. 'A fit agent is a fine agent' as one of our mottoes says, and the course will make you all familiar with the countryside around the camp. You will run up Mount Globe, around and back again. The track is clearly marked with yellow flags. You will represent your age divisions, and the first team with all members back will be awarded points for the Shining Stars competition."

EJ, CC and KM looked at each other excitedly. The Shining Stars competition was **SHINE**'s spy of the year award and agents were always keen to pick up extra points. EJ, CC and KM would be on the same team, the under-twelve team. Could they beat the older girls?

"There is one more thing," continued A1. "We have placed four objects along the course, objects that do not belong in the bush, that are out of place. A good agent, an agent on the ball, must notice things like this. Each team must correctly identify and take a photo of each of the four objects. Any team that finishes without finding them will be disqualified. Okay, now please line up at this first yellow flag."

The agents lined up, grouped in their teams, waiting. EJ looked at CC, who looked at KM, who looked at EJ. They were ready and determined to show what the under-twelves could do.

"Agents," cried A1, "are you ready? On your marks, get set, go!"

The agents ran out of the camp gates and into the bush. The race was on.

Chapter •6

EJ, KM and CC took off quickly, eager to make a good start, but it was hard work running on the dirt track. The path was uneven and every now and then it was blocked completely by boulders that the girls had to scramble over. Sometimes they hit jump mode on their shoes and jumped over them, but they were worried they might miss one of the objects if they did it too often. All the same, the running shoes were excellent and fun—cross-country running at school was never like this!

CC and KM were strong, fast runners and EJ had to work hard to keep up with them. She was also on the lookout for the four objects. She didn't have far to look for the first one—they had only been on the bush track for a little while when they saw something red in one of the trees. A quick bounce with the turbo shoes and the girls had found the first object—four red balloons tied to a tree.

"That has to be the first one," said CC, taking out her phone and snapping a photo. "This one was easy, everyone would have gotten it, let's keep going."

The track now pushed up the mountain, making the run harder, but using their shoes certainly helped. Even without the shoes, EJ was getting a lot of exercise. *This has to be good for my soccer,* she thought. They were nearly at the top of the hill, and out of breath, when they saw a pair of skis leaning against a tree.

"That has to be strange thing number two," said EJ. "There's no snow here."

The girls stopped to photograph the skis. Taking their water bottles from their packs, they had a drink.

Farther along the track, halfway down Mount Globe, EJ could see something moving through the trees. "We're doing well, but look, another group is ahead of us."

"How did they get there so fast?" cried CC, wiping her mouth and putting her bottle back in her pack.

"Let's go!" said KM.

The three girls took off again. EJ was finding the going much easier now that the track was heading downhill. She was even able to keep up with KM. She and KM had just scrambled over another big set of rocks when CC called them back. She was still on top of the rocks when she looked up and saw a rock ledge above her. There seemed to be something sticking out the side.

"Hold on, I think there is something up here," she cried to KM and EJ and pointed up to the ledge. CC climbed up a bit farther and there was a teddy bear sitting on a little rock.

"How cute!" exclaimed CC, taking a photo. "But it doesn't belong here: it must be object three."

"Good spotting, CC," said KM. "I climbed straight past that."

"That's why you are in the fast-transportation division and CC is in surveillance," said EJ, laughing. "Come on, we only have one more object to find."

The girls set off again. The track was not so steep now and they crossed a dry creek bed. As the girls ran across, they noticed a school crossing sign.

CC snapped the photo. "That makes four objects."

"Time to speed back to camp," said KM.

"Do you think we'll catch those older girls?" EJ asked.

"I'll use my shoes to check how far in front they are," said KM. She pressed the button with the arrow on it and jumped, bouncing high up into the trees and then grabbing on to a branch. "We're nearly at the bottom and that first group is only just ahead of us now," she cried. "Hold on, what's this? Come up here, guys."

CC and EJ looked at each other, slightly puzzled, but they pushed their shoes' buttons for jump mode and bounced. As they jumped up among the trees, they could see what KM had seen. There was something like a tree house in one of the trees at the bottom of the mountain near the clearing.

The girls leapt down and ran to find the tree. Just when they were about to give up, EJ found a tree with small pieces of wood nailed to the trunk. She called to the other girls.

"Guys, over here, I think this is a ladder!"

And it was. The girls climbed up and reached a wooden platform high up among the top branches of the tree. The same platform KM had spotted. It was a tree house.

"This is so cool," said CC. "It's a lookout. And see, the wood looks almost new. This hasn't been here long. Hey, look over there, you can see the enclosures near the camp fence." She took a charm from her bracelet and twisted it to produce a pair of binoculars.

"Cool charm," commented EJ. "Can you see anything?"

"Yes," cried CC. "I can see puppies! Look!"

CC passed the binoculars to EJ who looked and then passed them on to KM.

"Maybe A1 made a mistake," said EJ. "Maybe there were five things." She took a photo of the tree house with her phone.

"Make that six," said KM. "Check this out." She bent down and picked up a small, round metal disk with the **SHINE** logo on it.

"It looks like a dog tag," said EJ. "What's it doing up here? We'd better take it back with us."

"And we'd better get back if we want to have a chance of winning," added KM.

"No rush, we don't have a chance," said CC, looking across to the camp with her binoculars. "The other teams are already running back through the front gates."

"We lost time up here in the tree house," said EJ a little glumly.

"But if the other teams missed the tree house," KM pointed out, "we might still win on points. We only found it when I jumped to see how far we had to go. Come on, let's get back."

The girls carefully climbed back down the ladder and jumped onto the track. They ran the rest of the way down the mountain, out of the bush and through the gates, where A1 was waiting for them.

"Good job, girls," cried A1.

EJ pulled up, puffing. It didn't feel like a good job. She couldn't help being disappointed. They had come last, after all.

"Don't be too disappointed," said A1. "Remember you are the youngest agents. Now, before you go into dinner, did you find the four things?"

EJ brightened a little. "The balloons and the skis."

"Correct," confirmed A1.

"And the teddy bear and the school crossing," said CC.

"Well done," said A1 smiling.

"And the tree house and the dog tag," said KM.

"I beg your pardon," said A1. "What did you say, Agent KM12?"

"The tree house and the dog tag, A1," repeated KM.

"That's why we took so long," explained EJ. "We were up in the tree house. Look, we took a photo and we found this disk. We think it is a dog tag." EJ passed the tag to A1.

A1 wasn't smiling anymore. Her eyes had narrowed and her lips were pursed. For once, EJ knew what *she* was thinking.

"That wasn't part of the hunt, was it?" said EJ.

"No," said A1, "it wasn't."

For a moment no one spoke. Then EJ 's eyes widened as she realized what that meant.

"But if **SHINE** didn't build it, doesn't that mean someone outside **SHINE** knows the location of our camp?"

"Yes, EJ12, it does."

"*SHADOW*?"

"I don't know, EJ12. I hope not," said A1 grimly.

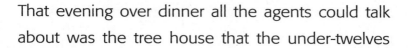

That evening over dinner all the agents could talk about was the tree house that the under-twelves had discovered. EJ, CC and KM were rather proud that they were the only ones that had spotted it. A1 had given them the same number of Shining Star points as the under-sixteens, who won the race. That made them even prouder. Everyone was talking loudly when A1 stood up at the front of the dining hall and tapped on her water glass with a spoon.

"Could I have your attention please, agents," said A1.

The room went quiet immediately.

"Thank you. The camp program will continue as planned but, in the light of today's discovery, all agents are to be on high alert. The older agents will now leave for their night camp. Be alert for any further signs of possible *SHADOW* activity in the area. The under-twelves need to get themselves to bed. They will report to Agent BRK9 in the morning for puppy training."

EJ, CC and KM blushed. The older agents were off to search for *SHADOW* agents and they were going to bed?

"How embarrassing!" said EJ, covering her face with her hands.

"Why did A1 have to say that?" groaned CC. "She made us seem like babies."

"Yes," agreed KM, "but," she continued stifling a yawn, "I *am* tired and we do need to be up early for puppy training."

"I can't wait," said EJ. "I wonder what work we will be doing with them?"

The girls left the dining hall and as they walked toward their sleeping cabin, they could see the older girls heading off for their bush camp.

"Lucky them," said EJ.

"I still wish we were going too," said CC. But she was yawning as she said it.

Each age group had its own cabin so it was EJ, CC and KM in one. They changed into their special **SHINE**-issue pajamas—long gray-and-white stripy pants and white T-shirt with the **SHINE** logo on it—and cleaned their teeth. Even the toothpaste had the **SHINE** logo on it. By the time they were done, EJ, CC and KM were all yawning and they almost fell into their beds. EJ lay on her back and pulled her blanket up toward her.

"Hey, this is just like a sleepover," said EJ. "What should we do?"

There was no reply.

"Guys, what should we do?"

There was still silence.

"Guys?"

Silence. Then she heard snores. Two different snores. KM and CC were fast asleep.

EJ yawned. *I'd better get some sleep too,* she thought. *Tomorrow will be a big day.*

EJ12 had no idea how big.

Chapter •7

The girls woke up early, rushed through their breakfast and tore over to the dog kennels in the far corner of the training camp. The dogs began barking loudly. There were some beautiful huskies and EJ recognized them immediately: they were the huskies that she had rescued from *SHADOW* agent Caterina Hill's Antarctica ice hotel. And, there were the puppies. The girls squealed again as they saw three little Labrador puppies, two golden and one black, all tumbling around playing with an old soccer ball in their pen. All the dogs had little

SHINE tags on their collars.

"These tags are the same as the one we found in the tree house," said EJ. "It was a dog tag. But how did it get up in the tree house?"

"Good question, EJ12," said a woman coming around the corner. It was Agent BRK9, the **SHINE** dog trainer. "None of our dogs are missing their tags. It's a mystery."

"Good morning, BRK9," said EJ. "May I say hello to the huskies?"

"Of course," said BRK9.

EJ went into the husky yard. The big dogs gathered around her as if they were greeting her. *Do they remember me from the South Pole?* she wondered, as she ran her hand through the long fur of one of the dogs.

"You're a good dog, aren't you?" she said, still patting the husky as she looked into its light-blue eyes. Then, as she stroked the dog, EJ felt something small and hard, almost like a little disk, under the fur on its shoulder. EJ called to BRK9. "What's this under the dog's fur? There's something hard."

BRK9 came straight over and felt the disk. "Oh, that's okay, it's only her microchip. Most dogs have them so you can trace them to their owner if they get lost. It doesn't hurt the dogs at all. Now, come and join the others and meet your training partners."

BRK9 opened the gate to the puppy pen and the girls went in. The puppies leapt all over them, licking and pawing them excitedly.

"They need some exercise," said BRK9, laughing. "Let's get the ball rolling—it's time for soccer."

"Soccer?" asked EJ, looking puzzled. "But I thought we were doing puppy training."

"You are, EJ12," replied BRK9. "Soccer is a great way to exercise the pups and to practice some of the commands they're learning. You'll see. Now, girls, please activate your high frequency whistle charm," said BRK9. "We use it for the puppies, along with a few voice commands."

The puppies were let out of the pen and they ran everywhere. When BRK9 blew her whistle, they stopped and sat down. BRK9 blew her whistle twice and the puppies began running around again.

EJ took the whistle charm from her bracelet and twisted. Then she removed the plug and placed it in her ear. CC and KM did the same. This time when BRK9 blew, they could hear a sharp whistle. And so could the puppies, who sat down again.

"EJ, you will be looking after Blackie, the little black puppy," explained BRK9. "CC, you will be with Bella, the golden lab with the black collar and, KM, you will be training Bessie, the golden lab with the blue collar. You will be playing soccer with the puppies. At any time, however, you may say the puppy's name and blow the whistle once. Then the puppy must stop and sit. This teaches them control: they must obey the command rather than continue to play with the ball. That's not easy for a puppy, so when they obey you must give them lots of praise. When you blow the whistle twice the puppy can continue playing. Although they're still young, they can understand quite complicated sequences of commands. Do any of you have the dog whisperer charm?"

"I do," said EJ, holding the bone-shaped charm.

Once twisted it became a jar of little dog treats that all dogs found irresistible.

"Excellent. Please activate it and give the other girls some chum chews." BRK9 threw the soccer ball up in the air. "Now, off you go!"

KM stretched up and immediately headed the ball to CC. EJ was impressed. The girls kicked the ball around, passing it to each other as the puppies joined in, chasing the ball from girl to girl and trying to grip it with their mouths.

EJ called, "Blackie!" and blew her whistle. The black pup stopped, looked at EJ and then sat.

"Good girl, Blackie, good girl," said EJ, giving the puppy a little treat. The ball rolled past and the puppy dived after it. "No, Blackie," said EJ. She hadn't blown the whistle twice so the puppy needed to stay sitting. Again EJ blew her whistle once. Now the puppy sat and was rewarded with another chum chew. Then EJ blew the whistle twice and Blackie took off, chasing the ball that was moving between KM and CC, with a little interruption from Bella and Bessie.

"Here, EJ," cried CC, "take the header!"

Oh no, thought EJ, *here we go again.* EJ leapt up to the ball, aiming her head at where she thought the ball was going. It wasn't. The ball sailed past and landed on Blackie's head. Even the puppy could do a header!

EJ must have looked a little discouraged because CC came up to her. "You nearly got it," she said. "But you do know the trick about heading the ball, don't you?"

EJ looked at her spy buddy. Was she joking? Did she look as if she knew the trick about heading the ball?

"No," said EJ, "I don't think I do."

"Don't look at where you want the ball to go. Keep your eye on the ball."

"On the ball?"

"Exactly. Then keep your chin in and hit the ball with your forehead in the direction you want the ball to go. Here, try again."

CC went back and kicked the ball up high toward EJ. EJ watched the ball and moved her head toward it. This time the ball made contact with her head, but then it just bounced off.

"That was better," said CC, "but you forgot to push. Now, kick me one."

EJ kicked the ball up in CC's direction. CC ran to meet the ball and then, as it was coming down, she jumped, her eyes always firmly on it. Her chin tucked in, CC stretched her neck and then met the ball with the middle of her forehead, pushing it back to EJ.

"That was great!" cried EJ.

"It's just practice," said CC. "I missed them all the time when I first tried."

"Hello, people, can we get back to the game?" cried KM.

CC laughed and kicked the ball toward KM, who didn't quite get to it before Bessie rushed in and took it.

"Bessie, sit," called KM, blowing the whistle once. The puppy sat.

"Good girl," said KM. "If only we could make other teams sit and stay the same way!"

The girls continued to play with the puppies and

EJ kept trying the headers—one even went in the right direction, although not to the right person. It was a start.

The puppies were doing well too. Sometimes they ran off before they were allowed to, but the girls made sure to make them sit again. It seemed everyone was getting better with practice. Then something strange happened.

Blackie was sitting. EJ blew the whistle to release her but accidentally blew three times rather than two. Blackie began running, but then ran all the way back into her kennel. She sat at the back of the pen looking over to the camp fence. It was as if she was waiting for something. EJ looked up to where Blackie seemed to be looking. She could just see the tree house in the distance. *Is that where the puppy was looking?* she wondered.

"Blackie!" called EJ. "Come!" She blew the whistle again, this time twice, and the puppy came back and began to play.

"Did you see that?" EJ asked CC.

"See what?" replied CC.

"Watch this," said EJ and she called Blackie's name then blew her whistle three times again. Sure enough, Blackie ran back into the dog kennel and sat by the fence looking out.

"What's she doing?" asked CC.

"I'm not sure," said EJ. "It's strange that Blackie looks toward the tree house when I whistle three times."

CC shrugged. "Maybe she'd just had enough."

"She did it twice, so I don't think so," replied EJ. "Let's tell BRK9."

BRK9 looked worried when EJ told her what had happened. "Hmm, we haven't taught them a three-whistle command yet. And Blackie has seemed out of sorts for the last little while, but I haven't been able to figure out why." She bent down and scratched Blackie behind the ears. "Thanks, EJ. I'm not sure what it means, but it might be important," she said, straightening up again. "But now it's time for your spy charm session with IQ400. You'll be seeing the puppies again later."

The girls gave the puppies a good-bye cuddle

and walked past the dog kennels toward the hall. As they were walking, EJ noticed a hole in the wire of the puppy pen where Blackie had sat, a hole big enough for a puppy to get through.

That was a strange thing, another strange thing. There were lots of strange things. The tree house and the extra dog tag, Blackie's strange behavior and now this hole. Were they all connected? EJ12 was starting to think they were.

Chapter · 8

When the girls walked into the dining room, IQ400 and A1 were standing behind a table. On the table was a row of metal boxes.

"These are charm chests," said A1. "You three are very lucky today. You are among the first **SHINE** agents to see the latest charms being developed in our laboratories. IQ400, what do you have for us?"

"I have a few charms which are just about to go into production. This first one is a personal favorite," said IQ, taking out a charm in the shape of a dolphin. "It is a dolphin trainer charm and it allows agents to work with dolphins. I am excited about this one: it could be an important breakthrough for us in underwater missions."

EJ's eyes were nearly popping out of her head. A dolphin trainer charm, how amazing was that? Although EJ wasn't so sure that she would like an underwater mission. She loved swimming, but she was a little bit nervous about deep water. She guessed that would probably rule her out of a marine mission, but you never could tell with SHINE.

"Daydreaming, EJ12?" asked IQ400, but not in an angry way.

"Oh, sorry," said EJ, blushing.

"Perhaps you need this?" IQ400 was holding a little bottle of a murky-colored liquid.

EJ didn't like the look of the drink. "Um, thanks, but I'm not thirsty."

"But are you thirsty for knowledge?" asked IQ400.

"To drink?" EJ was confused.

"Yes!" exclaimed IQ400. "A knowledge drink, a brain energy drink, a think drink! I call it TD1000.

Just as some drinks can deliver instant energy to our bodies, TD1000 will deliver energy to our brains."

EJ was still confused. "You mean a drink to make us think better?" she asked.

"Exactly!" cried IQ400 excitedly. "Can you imagine the great things we could do if we could use more of our brains, more quickly, more of the time? That is what TD1000 is going to do. We have been experimenting with different combinations of foods we know to be good for the brain, foods that help boost your memory."

EJ was hoping chocolate was going to be one of those.

"Cabbage, liver, egg yolks," continued IQ400. "These are some of the key ingredients. We haven't gotten the taste right yet."

"Can we try some?" asked KM, who was always interested in doing things more quickly.

EJ and CC looked at her. Was she serious? KM wanted to drink that?

"Oh no," exclaimed IQ. "It's not ready. There are still problems, too many kinks still in the drinks!"

"What do you mean, IQ?" asked CC.

"Well, at the moment the TD1000 seems to be having the exact opposite effect when you drink it. When someone drinks it at the moment, they act like a little child. The effect wears off after a while, but it is very perplexing. We have a lot more work to do. The next batch, however, is almost ready."

IQ400 went to the end of the table. "Now, where is that other charm?" she said, as she looked on the bench. As she continued to search she explained. "It's a soccer ball charm. With the huge success of cupcake-cam, we are rolling out, if you will pardon the pun, ball-cam." IQ400 looked worried. "That's strange. I am sure I left the charm here..."

"Perhaps you left it back in the lab at HQ?" asked A1, who now also looked worried.

"No, I am positive I packed it in a charm chest," said IQ. "It was right here last night."

EJ watched as IQ looked at A1 who looked at IQ. Both now looked worried. That made EJ worried. What was going on? Was this another strange coincidence? Was the ball-cam just missing? Or had it been taken? And, if it had been taken, who had taken it?

A1 finished the CHARM session early and canceled the afternoon training sessions on the dirt bikes. The girls were disappointed, but they realized that this was no longer a training camp: it had become a mission.

EJ, KM and CC spent the afternoon searching the entire campground for the missing charm chest. They looked everywhere, in all the cabins, in all the bushes, even in the dog kennels, but it was nowhere to be found.

EJ was walking around the perimeter fence line near the dog kennels. Looking up she could, again, make out the tree house. Once you knew what to look for it was easy to spot. But then, as EJ came closer, she saw something else. There in the camp fence, almost directly in line with the hole in the dog yard fence was another hole, another puppy-sized hole. EJ knelt down by the hole and there clearly, in the dirt on the other side of the fence, were prints, paw prints. Puppy-sized paw prints.

Chapter · 9

It was late evening, after dinner, and EJ, CC and KM had snuck back into the dining hall to see what they could find for their midnight feast. They might be secret agents, but that didn't mean they couldn't have some fun, and they wouldn't have been very good secret agents if they couldn't organize a secret midnight feast. They were just opening the pantry door when they heard barking. Puppy barking.

"The puppies should be asleep," said CC. There was more barking.

"Well, they're not asleep. Come on," said EJ. "We'd better check it out."

The three agents left the dining hall and dashed across to the dog kennels. The barking was getting louder.

EJ shone her flashlight into the puppies' pen but could only see Bella and Bessie, who barked again. "Where's Blackie?" she whispered to the others.

"She must be here," replied CC.

"Perhaps we just can't see her because her coat is so black," suggested KM.

Then EJ remembered the hole in the fence. "Quick," she whispered to the others, "come around here."

EJ ran around to the back of the pen where the hole was and shone her flashlight around. Blackie wasn't there and EJ didn't expect her to be. After watching her that morning during soccer training, she knew something strange was happening with the puppy and now she had gone.

CC and KM crept up behind her.

"EJ," CC whispered, "what have you found?"

"There's a hole," said EJ.

"Blackie must have gone through it," said KM.

EJ nodded.

"But where to?" asked CC.

"Let's check the camp fence," said EJ, turning away from the puppy pen. Then she stopped, as straight ahead of her a light began to flash. It wasn't CC or KM's flashlight because they were beside her with their flashlights still pointing at the hole in the puppy pen. This light was in front of her, a long way in front. It seemed to be coming from outside the camp.

"Hey, CC, KM, look at that light," she whispered. "Up in the trees."

KM and CC turned around.

"It's flashing on and off," said KM, "and hold on, isn't that where the tree house is?"

"Exactly," said EJ.

"Quick, turn your flashlights off or whoever it is will see you," said CC, turning off her own. The other girls did the same.

Luckily, the person outside the camp didn't seem to notice them because the flashlight kept flashing.

"See how sometimes it flashes quickly and sometimes it stays on for a while?" EJ told the others.

"Yes," said KM.

"Well," said EJ, "I think that someone is flashing a code."

"What sort of code?" asked KM.

"Morse code," replied EJ.

"A code?" cried CC. "But who would be sending it and, actually, who would they be sending it to? We are the only ones out here."

"No we're not," said EJ.

"We're not?" said KM a little nervously.

"No. Look straight ahead."

CC and KM turned and looked. There was a little light, flashing by the camp fence.

"What is that?" whispered KM.

"Look closer," said EJ.

"I can just make out the shape of something…" said KM.

"What on earth!" gasped CC. "It's Blackie."

"Yep," said EJ, "the little light is on her collar.

And notice that it's flashing with exactly the same pattern as the light from outside the camp."

"You're right," said CC.

"Blackie is receiving a message," said E J. "I'm sure of it. We need to copy down the flashes. We write a dot for a short flash and a dash for a long one. We have already missed some of the message, but we can still get the end. CC, can you please shine your flashlight on my notepad so I can write?"

"You carry a notepad?" asked CC, cupping her hand over the end of her flashlight so whoever was in the tree house wouldn't see it.

"Yes," said E J, "don't you?" She continued to write until the flashlight in the tree house suddenly stopped. "And now let's see what we have." E J looked at what she had written.

..—. . — —.—. .... —... ——— —..—

EJ opened the code app on her phone. She scrolled to Morse and pressed OK. The alphabet appeared on the screen.

```
A._        J.___  5...    2..___

B_...  K_._  T_      3...__

C_._.  L._..  U.._    4...._

D_..   M__   V..._    5.....

E.        N_.   W.__    6_....

F.._.  O___  X_.._    7__...

G__.   P.__.  Y_.__    8___..

H....  Q__._  Z__..    9____.

I..      R._.   1.____  0_____
```

84

"Now all we have to do is decode the message," said EJ. "Look at the first bit."

..—.

EJ checked the Morse code table.

"Two shorts, they're the two dots and one long, that's the dash, and then another short. I check the table and, see, that's an F," she said. "Then we do the next one, and it's just one dot, see?" EJ pointed to the part of the code.

"I think I get it," said KM. "The next one is just one long dash, so that's a T?"

"There are only two more letters to this first word, look," said EJ.

—.—. ....

"Long, short, long, short is C," continued EJ, "and the last one is four shorts. An H."

"So that makes F-E-T-C-H FETCH," said CC.

"Exactly," said EJ. "You could join the code-cracking division."

CC smiled.

"That was cool, EJ," exclaimed KM. "What does the last bit say?"

EJ quickly matched the last letters and showed her paper to KM and CC.

F E T C H   B   O   X
..—. . — —.—. ....   —... ——— —..—

"FETCH BOX," said CC. "But what does it mean?"

"And why would you send a code message to a dog?" said KM. "It doesn't make any sense. You might be able to crack the code, EJ, but a puppy couldn't."

Then the girls heard something. A voice, and it was coming from where Blackie was sitting near the camp fence.

"BLACKIE, FETCH BOX."

"I know that voice," said EJ.

"So do I," said CC.

"Me too," gulped KM.

And the girls all felt a sudden chill down their spines. Or should that be a CHill? The voice was that of Dr. C. Hill, Dr. Caterina Hill, the evil *SHADOW* scientist. EJ had met her once before, and so had CC and KM. Caterina was scary and Caterina was mean, very mean. None of the agents fancied going head to head against Caterina again.

The girls might have heard her voice, but Caterina wasn't there.

"Where is she?" whispered KM.

"I don't know," said EJ, "but look, Blackie is running toward the dining hall, and listen."

"Blackie, Fetch Box."

"That's Caterina again," said CC.

"No," said EJ, "it's Caterina's voice and it's coming from where Blackie is."

"And now look," whispered CC. "Blackie is going into the dining room."

The girls watched, stunned, as the puppy pushed the dining room door open and went in, coming out seconds later, with a little black box in her mouth. The puppy ran to the fence and then disappeared from view. The girls ran to the dining room.

"One of the charm chests is gone! That's what Blackie was carrying," cried KM.

"Blackie is the spy? That cute little puppy is a spy?" asked CC sadly.

"No, not Blackie," said EJ. "It's Caterina, she's making Blackie do it. Somehow she is sending Blackie messages remotely."

"And now, Blackie's coming back," said KM, shining her flashlight out the dining room door. Sure enough the puppy seemed to be making her way back toward the dog kennels. She was no longer carrying the charm chest.

"Blackie," called EJ. "Come here, that's a good girl."

EJ picked up the little puppy, who looked up into EJ's eyes and gave her a little lick. EJ stroked Blackie's head and tickled behind her ears and it was then that she noticed the dog tag.

"Hey, guys," said EJ, "look at this."

"It's a dog tag," said KM.

"Yes," said EJ, "but this tag is different from the others. It's thicker and heavier. We need to show it to A1 and IQ400. We need to tell them everything."

"Yes," agreed KM, "but perhaps we should leave out the bit about the midnight feast?"

Chapter • 10

EJ, KM, CC and Blackie were in the camp office with A1, BRK9 and IQ400. IQ400 had been looking at Blackie's collar.

"It's clever, very clever," she said. "This may look like our standard-issue dog tag, but it's anything but standard. Behind the **SHINE** logo, Caterina has hidden a device that can not only receive and process light flashes as Morse code, it can also then convert that Morse code into simple voice commands. The same simple voice commands that Blackie has been trained to obey. Listen." IQ400 pushed a button inside the tag.

"Blackie, Fetch Box." It was Caterina's voice again.

EJ shuddered. "I thought Caterina was in **SHINE** prison, A1?"

"She was until a month ago," explained A1. "She managed to escape and then she disappeared. We couldn't find her anywhere."

"But how did she find the **SHINE** camp?" asked CC. "You said you moved its location every month."

"I think I know the answer to that," said EJ. "The huskies we rescued from Caterina's polar plant have microchips. I bet Caterina also implanted homing devices within the chips. So when Caterina escaped, the first thing she did was locate the dogs. If she could find the dogs, she could find **SHINE**."

"I'd say you're right, EJ12," said A1.

"But what I don't understand," said EJ, "is why Caterina didn't use her huskies. Why did she use Blackie?"

"I can help there, A1," said BRK9. "The huskies might be too obvious, and who would suspect puppies? As you know, we found the puppies outside the camp a month ago. We thought they had been abandoned, but now I don't think that's the case. I think Caterina had already trained them and then left them for us to find."

EJ was angry. "She just left the puppies? What if we hadn't found them? They would have starved."

"But we did find them," said A1. "Unfortunately, by taking them in we also let Caterina into the camp. But one thing still puzzles me: we know that Caterina goes to the tree house, but how does she call Blackie?"

E J remembered what had happened that morning. "She whistles three times. That's Blackie's instruction to come first to the hole in the dog pen and then to the hole in the camp fence."

"How do you know that, EJ?" asked A1.

"Because when I blew my whistle three times by mistake, Blackie went straight to the fence."

"Well done again, EJ," said A1 approvingly.

"And once Blackie is there," continued CC, "Caterina uses a flashlight to flash the message. The special dog tag converts the flashes into commands for Blackie."

"And the command is FETCH BOX," said E J. "That must mean the charm box."

"Yes!" cried KM. "And then Blackie brings the charm box to Caterina."

"And last night she took the TD1000 charm box," said A1. "Well done, girls."

"But where did she go?" asked E J. "Where is Caterina now? She knows where we are, but how will we find out where she is?"

"I wonder…" said A1.

"I'll get those fences fixed," said IQ400.

"No," said A1 suddenly, "don't fix anything. I have a better idea. I think we will lay a little trap for Caterina."

A trap? E J, CC and KM suddenly brightened. They were going to set a trap for Caterina.

"This will be an extremely difficult mission," continued A1. "I wonder if we can get one of the older divisions back in time?"

"No!" EJ cried.

"You can't!" cried CC.

"We can!" cried KM.

"I beg your pardon?" said A1, clearly taken aback.

"Sorry, A1," said EJ. "I mean, we mean, we can do this. After all, I've stopped Caterina once before and we did discover what she is up to. We can stop her again."

A1 looked at her three youngest agents and smiled. "Well, the other agents are a long way away..."

"Please, A1," said EJ. "We can do this."

"Yes," said A1, "I think you can. Okay then, listen carefully. Here's the plan."

Chapter · 11

It was early the next evening. Everyone was in position. Waiting. That was the plan. They would wait for Caterina to call Blackie again. There were two charms left and she was sure to come for them. When she did, **SHINE** would be ready for her.

EJ, CC and KM would be able to follow Blackie to Caterina. EJ was just outside the dog kennels. She would watch Blackie go to the fence and then decode the Morse message. They expected the same FETCH BOX command but needed to make sure. CC was on lookout near the dining hall to watch

Blackie take the charm and KM was positioned at the camp gate ready to take the lead in following Blackie. Both EJ and CC would follow behind KM. A1, BRK9 and IQ400 were in a hastily assembled mission command in the kitchen.

The girls had been fitted out with night-mission gear. Dressed in black with night goggles and head flashlights, they would also be able to talk to each other via spy-talkers, special ear and mouthpieces that fit around their heads. Once activated, you simply talked as usual. The spy-talkers also had a homing device so that A1 and IQ400 could track the girls and follow them on IQ400's laptop. The girls weren't the only ones with a homing device: IQ400 had also put one into Blackie's tag. By the time Caterina realized it was there, it would be too late. EJ also had a **SHINE** special-issue, night-light pen, a pen with a flashlight, just what she would need for nighttime code cracking. Everything was ready.

The girls were nervous. This was no longer a drill. It was real—no more teddy bears on rock ledges but Caterina Hill in a tree house, and Caterina Hill was certainly no cute teddy bear. She would let nothing—and no one—stand in her way.

But then EJ remembered that someone had stood in Caterina's way and had stopped her evil scheme. She had.

I've beaten her before, EJ told herself, *and I will again.* All the same, the waiting in the dark made her a bit jumpy. It would be good to get going. EJ checked her equipment: her spy-talker was in place and her whistle charm was secure in the other ear. She turned her head flashlight off and waited. She was ready.

Then they heard it. Three sharp whistles coming from the direction of the tree house. It was Caterina. It was time.

"Good luck, KM and CC," whispered EJ into her spy-talker. "We can do this."

"You too," came KM's voice. "Of course we can do this. Here come the under-twelves."

EJ watched, her pen and notepad ready. Within seconds Blackie had slipped through the hole in the pen and padded over to the camp fence. A few seconds later, there was a light from high in the trees outside the camp fence. The light began flashing. EJ worked quickly, writing the message down. As she wrote, she could tell it wasn't the same command as last time.

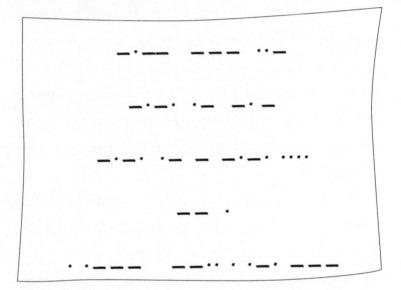

"Guys, we may have a problem," EJ whispered into her spy-talker. "There is something different about this message."

"What?" whispered KM back.

"Well," said EJ, "it starts with YOU, not BLACKIE and then..."

"EJ?" whispered CC, "what then?"

EJ had stopped talking while she worked out the next word. "And then the next word is C-A-N-T, which means CAN'T. The first two words are YOU CAN'T."

"You can't? Who can't?" said CC. "What does that mean? It doesn't sound like a dog command."

"Quick, EJ," said KM, "we need the rest of the code."

EJ worked furiously, quicker than she had ever decoded a message before, but as she did, she started to feel sick. It was almost as if CC and KM could feel something was wrong.

"EJ, what is it?" said KM.

"Guys," broke in CC, "something's wrong. Blackie's not moving. I don't think she understands the command."

"Oh no," cried EJ. "Blackie might not, but I do." She had just cracked the code.

"What is it, EJ?" said KM.

"It's not good," said EJ, looking down at what she had written.

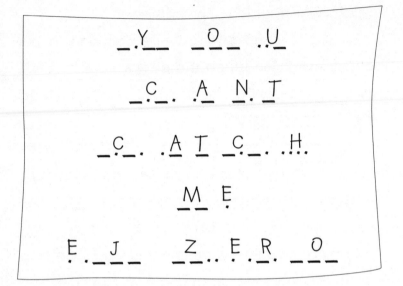

_.Y_ _O_ .U_

_C_. A N T

_C_. .A I _C_. .H.

M E

E J Z E R O

"It says, YOU CAN'T CATCH ME EJ ZERO. Caterina knows we're trying to trap her. Our plan won't work!"

"But she might still be in the tree house," cried KM. "Quick, if we run we can still catch her!"

The three girls ran headlong out the gate and along the track toward the tree house. KM, who had been on lookout at the camp gate, had a good head start.

"I'm nearly at the tree," she panted into the spy-talker. "About another hundred yards."

"We're right behind you," cried EJ, as she ran. Her legs were hurting, but there was no way she was stopping now. She switched to speed boost on her shoes and shot along the track. CC came up beside her.

"Let's go, EJ. One more speed boost and we will be at the tree."

"I'm here," KM's voice came over the spy-talker.

A1's voice came through on the spy-talkers. "Do not approach Caterina by yourself. Wait until you are all there."

EJ and CC hit the speed boost and in seconds they were at the bottom of the tree with KM. They switched to jump mode and all jumped together. Up toward the tree house and Caterina Hill.

BOING!

They landed on the platform. But there was no one there. Caterina had gone. There was, however, a note pinned to the tree, a note written in sharp, pointy handwriting.

Told you so,
EJ zero

"We're too late," said KM glumly. "Caterina's escaped. She even had time to leave a note."

"But how? Where?" said EJ. "We would have seen her running away, wouldn't we? Where could she have gone?"

"This way," said CC, who had been looking around the other side of the tree. "We must have missed this last time."

CC had found a zip line, a strong steel cable leading steeply down from the tree to—to where? They couldn't see, but the cable was definitely connected to something at the other end.

"What are we waiting for?" cried KM. "Let's follow it!"

"But we don't know where it goes," said EJ.

"There's only one way to find out," said CC. "But Caterina will have the trolley at the other end. How will we travel on it?"

"Activate our rope charms," said EJ. "We can use the rope as a trolley. Here, I'll show you." EJ took her rope charm and twisted it. As the rope began to glow, EJ looped it over the zip line.

"Will the cable hold us?" asked CC.

"It held Caterina," said EJ. "Let's go."

EJ went first. She held on to her rope, pushed off the platform and, whoosh, the rope glided along the steel, speeding EJ down and through the trees. She felt the zip line straighten up and as it did, it began to slow down. EJ was approaching another tree and another platform. Had Caterina built a network of tree houses?

EJ let go of the rope and jumped, landing with a thump on the platform. Seconds later, KM and CC landed as well. The girls looked around. This platform was much bigger than the first and had a roof and walls, almost like a little room. And in the middle of the floor was a chair, a large, white, egg-like swivel chair with its back to the girls. EJ gasped. She remembered that chair. She knew who would be sitting on it.

"Thanks for dropping in yet again, EJ12. I've been expecting you and your little friends."

The chair spun around. It was Caterina Hill. She was just as EJ remembered her: tall with straight, almost-white blond hair pulled back from her long narrow face. A cold, mean-looking face with black eyes and eyebrows arched in two thin black lines. Caterina was wearing a tight black sweater over camouflage combat pants, and at the end of her long fingers were long, almost clawlike nails, painted dark green. Little Blackie was sitting in her lap. The puppy moved to go to EJ, but Caterina yanked her back. Blackie yelped.

Chapter · 12

"I'll take your spy-talkers, thank you, children. We wouldn't want A1 to ruin our little tree party, would we?" said Caterina in a cold, clipped voice. "Give them to me."

EJ, KM and CC stood still.

"Give them to me now," repeated Caterina, "or I will throw the dog out of the tree house."

"You wouldn't," gasped CC.

"She would," said EJ, taking off her spy-talker.

"Yes, I would indeed," said Caterina, taking the three spy-talkers. "What do I care about a puppy?

But since you have obeyed me, I will just throw these instead." With a flourish Caterina threw the spy-talkers over the edge of the tree house.

Blackie broke loose and ran to EJ, who quickly scooped her up.

"That makes four standing on the trapdoor," laughed Caterina.

Trapdoor? EJ, KM and CC looked down at the floor.

Caterina took a remote control from her pocket. "One push of this remote," she said, "and you will all fall down, a long way down. I don't need you, I already have enough **SHINE** knickknacks."

And then CC nudged EJ and gave a tiny nod toward a table made out of a section of cut logs. On it were some black boxes and a soccer ball and a little bottle. CC nudged EJ again and Caterina saw.

"Oh so you noticed that, did you, CC?" said Caterina. "Clever you. Yes, I have IQ400's precious charms. Well, they were IQ's, but now they are mine. You see, I am an evil inventor and evil inventors must have inventions to sell, but thanks to little Miss

106

EJ Zero here, I have been out of action for a while. So, I stole some of **SHINE**'s and now I will sell them instead."

"You can't do that," said KM. "They are not yours, they belong to **SHINE**."

"Don't be so ridiculous, you silly girl," laughed Caterina. "Finders, keepers. Anyway, I'm not selling them all."

"You're not?" said EJ.

"No, I am keeping this one all for myself," said Caterina, picking up the little bottle from the table. "I am not sharing TD1000 with anyone. I am already cleverer than everyone, but imagine how much cleverer I will be when I drink this. No one will be able to keep up with me. My plans will be so brilliant they will be unfathomable to mere ordinary people. I will rule the world!" And with that, Caterina pulled the stopper from the bottle.

"I really wouldn't drink that if I were you, Dr. Hill," said EJ.

"Oh wouldn't you, EJ Zero? Who's going to stop me?"

Caterina put the bottle to her lips. As the girls watched, she began to drink. First she closed her eyes then she wrinkled her nose, as if she were about to sneeze, then she looked as if she was going to spit the murky drink out. But she didn't. She drank the whole bottle.

Setting the bottle on the table, Caterina burped. Then she giggled and turned to the girls with an enormous grin on her face.

"Hi, I'm Caty," she said in a little girl's voice. "I wanna play! Will you big girls play with me?"

Caterina began to play with her hair, twisting it in her fingers. EJ, CC and KM watched, stunned. The TD1000 had turned Caterina's mind into that of a three-year-old, at least for now.

"Want to play ball with me?" asked Caty, and she picked up the ball-cam and threw it at CC's feet.

"Quick, CC," shouted KM moving off the trapdoor and toward Caterina, "the ball-cam, it's going to roll out of the tree house!"

CC managed to stick her foot out, but rather

than stopping the ball she kicked it straight up in the air, above EJ.

"EJ, use your head," cried CC.

"Watch the ball, EJ," shouted KM.

EJ jumped, still holding on to Blackie and keeping her eyes locked on the ball. She arched her back and stretched her head up toward the ball. She met it perfectly and headed it across to KM, who caught it. Ball-cam was safe. And, EJ realized, she had done a perfect header.

"That was fun!" said Caty, clapping her hands. "Will you take me home now please?" said Caty. "I want to go night-night."

"No problem," said EJ. "I think we know somewhere where you can get plenty of rest."

She passed Blackie to CC and took Caty's hand to help her climb down the ladder to the ground. She never imagined that she would be holding Caterina's hand!

CC and KM collected the stolen charms and they even found the spy-talkers in the bushes below. One was still working. CC used it to call A1 and let her know what had happened.

"Will you be my friend?" said Caty, as they walked down the track.

"Let's not push things," said EJ.

Chapter • 13

It was late when EJ, CC, KM and Blackie arrived back at camp with their new "little friend," but the whole camp was there to greet them. People were a little surprised to see Caterina skipping along, but EJ quickly explained.

"Interesting," said IQ400, "a very interesting reaction. We have never seen what happens when someone drinks a whole bottle." She took Caterina's hand. "Come with me. I've got some nice toys for you to play with in this van."

"Oh goodie," squealed Caty, giggling as she took

IQ400's hand. "Bye-bye, EJ. See you later!"

"Bye-bye, Caty!" cried EJ, as she watched IQ put Caty into the van. "A lot later, I hope," she said quietly.

"Here are the spy charms, A1," said CC, handing them over.

"And the spy-talkers," said KM.

"Well done, girls," said A1. "You kept your heads and saved the day. Who knows what we would have done if all those inventions fell into the wrong hands."

"We nearly lost the ball-cam," said CC, "but EJ saved it."

EJ blushed. "We all did," she said, "it was a team effort."

"Go on, say how you saved it," said KM, who looked proudly at her spy-buddy.

"It was nothing," insisted EJ. "Just something off the top of my head."

A1 looked puzzled, but the girls all laughed.

"Well, however you did it, we're proud of you, all of you," said A1. "I don't think the older divisions will mind when I tell you the winner of the Shining Star Camp points is the under-twelve division."

The other agents began to cheer. EJ, KM and CC couldn't stop smiling.

"And we have something else for you," continued A1, holding three little charms. "I think you also deserve your dog-trainer charms. They aren't spy charms, they are more like a certificate, an award for achievement. **SHINE** awards them for exceptional results in different areas and I think you three qualify."

"Thanks, A1!" cried the girls in unison. They immediately put the charms on each of their bracelets. Now they would have something that reminded them of their mission together as well, almost like a friendship charm, a spy-buddy charm.

"And now it is past everyone's bedtime," said A1. "It's been a big day."

The girls walked back to their cabin arm in arm.

"We never did get to have our midnight feast," said EJ.

"I know," said CC. "Maybe next time."

"Or maybe right now," cried KM. "Look!"

On the table in their cabin was a cake, a chocolate cake with chocolate icing. There was writing in icing on the top.

Well done, under-twelves!

Time for your feast!

"How did A1 know about our feast?" cried CC.

"I don't know, but I'm pleased she did!" said EJ. "Let's eat!"

The three girls sat in their pajamas, eating cake and talking about the mission.

"Your header in the tree house was awesome, EJ," said KM. "You did it perfectly."

"I couldn't have done it without your help, CC," said EJ, serving her friend another slice of cake.

"Hey, do you think A1 will let us go on missions together now?" asked CC.

"I hope so," said EJ.

"Me too," said KM.

"She won't if you don't go to bed now," said A1, poking her head around the door. But she was smiling. "Go to sleep now, Shining Stars."

And the three girls did. Their heads had barely touched their pillows and they were fast asleep. EJ was so fast asleep that she didn't notice that Blackie had made one final night walk: the little puppy had again crawled out of the hole in the fence, but this time to their cabin and EJ's bed. The little puppy jumped up and snuggled into EJ, who turned over, smiling in her sleep.

With the unexpected mission over, the girls spent the last morning of the camp playing soccer with the puppies and, much to their delight, riding through the bush on dirt bikes. Agent REV1 showed the girls how to work the gears and accelerator and, after a few wobbly starts and jolty gear changes, EJ, KM and CC were scooting around the camp and then out along the Mount Globe track. KM had a knack for finding puddles to ride through and the girls returned to the camp much muddier than when they had left.

"That was so much fun," said EJ, as she took off her helmet and bike jacket. "Let's go around the track one more time!"

But there wasn't time as the train back to **SHINE** and home would soon be leaving. The girls barely had time to give the puppies one more cuddle before joining the other agents and heading back up the mountain to the railway platform.

The train ride home was definitely quieter than the one to camp, but EJ, CC and KM still had lots of energy to chat and swap apps and phone numbers. They chose a special ringtone so they would know when it was one of them calling.

"I'm going to miss you guys," said EJ.

"Me too," said CC.

"Me three," said KM.

"Maybe A1 will send us all on a mission one time?" said EJ.

The girls all smiled at each other. How good would that be?

"Good luck with the soccer tryouts, EJ," said KM. "You will be great, I know you will."

The soccer tryouts. Tomorrow. EJ had forgotten about them, but now that she remembered, she wasn't worried at all.

Chapter • 14

Emma was at school early the next day. She wasn't the only one. Lots of kids had turned up before school for the tryouts.

Ms. Tenga blew her whistle. "I think we'll play girls versus boys again. That seemed a good, close game last time. Okay, everyone in position, let's play!" Ms. Tenga blew her whistle again and the game was on.

It seemed that everyone trying out had been practicing. Everyone seemed better: running hard, precision kicking, reading the play. After twenty minutes, neither team had scored.

"Five more minutes," cried Ms. Tenga. "Let's see if we can get a result in this game."

Isi had the ball. She passed it to Emma who kicked it to Hannah. Hannah started to run, but Oskar was catching up. Hannah kicked the ball to Elle, but Edvard was right behind her so she kicked it quickly on to Isi. Now it was Isi's turn to run and she powered up the field. No one could catch her. Isi was in front of the goal. She stopped for a moment, then kicked. A big, beautiful strong kick into the goal. She was going to score. At least she was until Oliver threw himself at the ball and deflected it out of the goal.

"Bad luck, Isi," cried Ms. Tenga. "Great kick, but what a stop, Oliver! Two minutes of play."

"Don't worry, Is, that was a brilliant kick," Emma called to her friend.

"Yeah, but Oliver's stop was better," Isi yelled back, as she returned to position. "Let's go, Em. I know we can win this."

Emma loved the way her friend just bounced

back when things went wrong. Bounce back, just like the ball coming toward Emma. Oliver had thrown the ball in, but Elle had intercepted it on its way to Edvard. She passed it quickly to Emma who kicked it on to Isi. This time Isi was being crowded. There was no way she could get clear to shoot for the goal, but she managed to kick it high, right up in front of the goal. Right up in front of Emma.

Emma knew exactly what to do. She arched her back and stretched her neck, keeping her eye on the ball the whole time. The ball came down and Emma met it perfectly. She pounded it into the goal. Oliver didn't have a chance this time.

Girls 1, Boys 0. Girls uncontrollably happy.

"Great game, everyone. The team will be on the bulletin board at lunchtime," said Ms. Tenga.

Lunchtime seemed to take forever to come, but when it finally did, the girls raced to the bulletin board.

"Yes!" cried Isi, as she ran her finger down the list of names. "You, you, you and..." Isi was about to burst, "and me! We're all on the team. We're all getting shirts with our names on them and we're all awesome! And my number is 4, my lucky number, and that is incredibly awesome too!"

Emma wondered how they were going to calm Isi down for afternoon class. She also wondered what her number was. She looked at the list, found her name, then ran her finger across to look up her number. It was number 12.

Perfect! she thought to herself. *After all, I made the team with a little help from CC, KM and EJ12!*

Emma Jacks and EJ12 return in

BOOK 7
MAKING WAVES

Did you miss Books 1 and 2?

In Hot & Cold, EJ must work out who is melting the ice in Antarctica.

In Jump Start she needs to stop SHADOW building a new spy satellite and save the rain forest animals.

That's the easy part ...

Did you miss Books 3 and 4?

In In the Dark, EJ12 needs to save the SHINE solar energy station.

In Rocky Road, she has to find out how SHADOW is sending out its messages and what it has to do with a rock concert.

That's the easy part ...

Did you miss Book 5?

SHADOW is cooking up a new invention
which could put SHINE in a real jam.
It's a recipe for disaster.
Special Agent EJ12 needs to be
patient and keep her eyes peeled.
She must get inside the chocolate cake
bakery, find out what is going on and
stop SHADOW's plan.

That's the easy part.
As EJ12, Emma Jacks can do anything.

So why is the school fund-raiser such a
problem?

Perhaps it isn't after all...